The Virtue of
Honesty

Pinocchio

Adapted by Elizabeth Brooke
Illustrated by David Austin Clar

ISBN: 0-7853-7306-3

One day a poor old woodcarver named Geppetto saw a bluebird resting on a log. "This magic log can make your dreams come true," whistled the bird.

"From this log, I'll make a marionette that can laugh and dance!" thought Geppetto. He whittled away at the wood until finally he was done. For the finishing touch, Geppetto painted a broad red smile on the marionette's face. "I'll call you Pinocchio," said Geppetto. "You'll be a good boy, won't you, Pinocchio?" he asked.

"Oh, yes!" crowed Pinocchio. Then he darted out the door!

As he ran, Pinocchio's nose began to grow. He didn't know it, but his nose grew because he had told a lie. He had already broken his promise to be good.

A policeman saw Pinocchio dashing down the street and grabbed him by the nose. "You should be in school," he scolded.

"Why, I'm just on my way to school!" lied Pinocchio. His nose grew a little more.

An out-of-breath Geppetto appeared just in time to overhear Pinocchio. Geppetto was delighted to hear that Pinocchio was going to school. He didn't know that the marionette wasn't telling the truth.

Geppetto handed Pinocchio a shiny coin. "Take this money and buy a book for school," he said. "I am so proud of you!"

Pinocchio was touched that Geppetto wanted to help him. Pinocchio resolved to be good, and his nose shrank back down to normal size. He set out to buy his book.

On the way to the bookstore, Pinocchio met a lame fox and a blind cat. Pinocchio did not know that they were thieves.

"Pssst!" called the thieves. "If you bury your coin here and go away for a bit, it will grow into a money tree. Then you'll have a hundred coins instead of just one!"

As he thought about the hundred coins, Pinocchio forgot all about his schoolbook. He dug a hole at once, buried his coin, then went away. When he came back, all that was left was an empty hole! The cat and fox had tricked him. They had stolen the coin.

Just then Pinocchio heard a bird singing. He looked up to see the bird turn into a beautiful fairy. "Pinocchio," she said, "if you are good and obey Geppetto, one day you'll become a real boy!" She swung Pinocchio onto her back and flew him home.

"I'll be good from now on," said Pinocchio. But Pinocchio soon broke his promise.

Pinocchio was on his way to school the next day when a boy called out to him, "Why go to school when you can play? Come with me to Playland!"

"I don't know," stammered Pinocchio. "I want to be a good boy."

"To be a bad boy you have to break rules. You can't break rules in Playland because there are no rules," said the boy.

This made sense to Pinocchio, so he went with the boy. Playland turned out to be a wonderful place. Boys ran through the streets minding no one but themselves, playing every day from dawn to dusk.

One year from the day he first arrived in Playland, Pinocchio awoke to find that he had sprouted donkey ears and a tail! "What has *hee-haw* happened to me?" he gasped.

A sweet whistle reached Pinocchio's ears. He looked up and saw the fairy. "All bad boys turn into donkeys sooner or later," she explained in a sad voice.

"Oh, I want to be a good boy!" cried Pinocchio. "I want to go home!"

"I see that you are truly sorry," said the fairy. "I will take away your ears and tail but I cannot take you home. Your father has been searching for you, and he is lost at sea."

"I will search the sea until I find him!" said Pinocchio. After several days of swimming, Pinocchio was swallowed by a giant whale. The scared marionette floated down into the whale's stomach.

"Is someone there?" said a quiet voice. A match flared, and Pinocchio saw Geppetto.

"I found you!" cried Pinocchio. As father and son embraced, the great whale's stomach shook violently.

Suddenly, Pinocchio and Geppetto were hiccupped out of the whale. They swam back to the shore. Pinocchio heard a whistle and looked up to see the bluebird. "All your misdeeds are forgiven, brave Pinocchio," she sang. "Be a good boy from now on."

At once Pinocchio felt different. He had become a real live boy! In that moment Pinocchio's heart was transformed as well, and he was a good and truthful boy forever after.

Honesty

Honesty means telling the truth, and it is always best to tell the truth. Pinocchio learned the hard way about the importance of being honest. When he told lies, everyone could tell. He also paid a big price for his dishonesty.

When you tell the truth, things will work out for the best. Honesty is the best policy!